HER GUARDIAN ANGEL

CHAPTER ONE

Salem

I'm running.

My breath comes in heavy pants as I force my legs to move faster. My arms pump hard as hair flies wildly around my face. I look quickly behind me, trying to see how close he is but I can barely see three feet in front of me. It's a crescent moon tonight and not a lot of light is filtering in through the treetops.

I hear footsteps thudding behind me and run faster through the woods, dodging bushes and trees as I go. I jump over a fallen tree branch, hitting the ground and stumbling. I fall down and my hands and knees sink into the cold mud. I push myself up to keep going but the mud is thicker than I expected and I lose my shoes as I try to scramble out of it. I can hear him crashing through the woods after me and he's close. There's no time to waste so I leave the shoes and take off barefoot.

I'm not sure which direction I'm running in anymore but I pray I'm going the right way. My house was in the middle of nowhere and I was never allowed to leave the grounds but I used to walk along the fence when I was younger and I know where the low spots are; where I'll be able to jump over. I've been waiting for this day, plotting and planning, for months now. That was when I learned that my father wasn't going to let me leave when I turned 18. I had been naïve to think that he would. He wouldn't even let me go into town with him, so I should have known that he wouldn't just let me go.

I've been trapped in that house my whole life. My mother died in childbirth with me and it's been just me and my father ever since. He's been strict and suffocating my whole life but when I was younger, I didn't know any better. As I got older, I realized how lonely I was. I wanted friends, a social life, maybe a boyfriend. I begged and pleaded with my father to stop homeschooling me and to let me go to school in town but he always said no.

I grew up in an old farmhouse that's seen better days. The house is two stories with a sagging roof and porch. The house is falling apart and in need of a ton of repairs and the barn located a couple of yards away from the back door is in even worse condition. Our house is settled smack dab in the middle of a couple acres with nothing around for miles. It used to be a working farm but after my mother's death, my father must have let everything drop.

Instead, his focus was solely on me. You'd

think that would be a good thing. A loving father doting on his only daughter, but it's not like that. For one thing, he's not that loving. He's strict and overbearing and he has made sure to get drunk and tell me every day that I killed my mother. It doesn't matter that I had no control over what happened, that I was literally being born. My father just could never see past my mother's death to me.

I'm smart, all I had to do around the house was read after all, but that also means that I'm smart enough to know that I'm naïve about a lot of stuff. I don't understand how the real world works, not really, and I'm desperate to learn about it. To make connections. I'm terrible in social situations and I've only had one friend my entire life. The boy I used to walk the fence with.

Campbell McConnely. I met him when I was just a girl. I had been six and wandering along the fence in the woods marking our property from the farm next door when I had run into him. He was older, ten at the time, and the most handsome boy that I had ever seen. He had wandered along his side of the fence with me and we had talked for hours until I had to go back home. He had met me the next day and the next until it became our thing. We would meet every day at 5 pm and walk the fence until it got too dark to see.

He was my first and only friend but he was also so much more. He was my closest confidante, the person I could tell all of my secrets too. He was my first crush and when I was sixteen, he became my first kiss. He was the first and only person I ever said I love you too. I used to picture us growing up and getting married. He had postponed college, opting to wait until I graduated and we could go together. Everything was on track until my father caught us one night a year ago. We had been standing at the fence, holding hands, when he had come through the trees and spotted us. My father had lost it and Campbell had tried to explain that we loved each other, that he would never hurt me but my father just dragged me away. From that day forward, I wasn't allowed out of the yard, I wasn't allowed out of my father's sight.

As soon as I knew that he was going to keep me trapped there indefinitely, I knew that I needed to figure out a way to escape. I've been trying to remember the layouts and best path to take for weeks now. Since I'm only allowed out in the yard and my father won't let me out of his sight, I couldn't go too close to the woods to really look around. I'm only allowed one hour of outside time and I had to make it count so I would jog the perimeter, over and over again, straining my eyes to see as far into the woods as I could.

I've got everything planned and I've been working to make sure that I'm successful. I've been running more, trying to build up my endurance and I've kept a little duffle bag tucked away with some of my clothes in it. Dresses, because that's the only thing my father lets me wear. Everything was ready to go. I just needed to wait until I could leave.

Today was my birthday. Eighteen and legally allowed to be on my own. I had waited until my father had gone to bed with a bottle of his favorite booze before I pulled up a loose floorboard and crawled out. My father had to move me down to the first floor when some of the stairs started to go and I'm lucky that he did. Not just because I would have fallen through the stairs by now, but because I was able to find a way out of this house. There are bars on the windows and all of the floorboards creak, so I never would have made it out of this house any other way. Not without waking my father up.

He had heard me anyways and I had heard him as he jumped out of bed, already calling my name. My duffle bag had snagged on a nail and by the time I had torn it free, he was coming out of his bedroom. I had taken off running towards the north but now I only had a short head start. I'm faster than him though and I'm hoping that it will be enough to get away.

I keep running north through the woods, my bare feet slapping as they hit a random mud puddle or twig. I sprint through the woods, ignoring the stabbing pain in my feet from stepping on rocks or other debris. I can feel the mud as it squishes between my toes and I can already tell that it's covering most of my legs. My thin dress flits around my thighs as my legs push harder. I can feel my heartbeat pounding in my chest, can hear it thumping in my ears. I see a light in the distance and I head in that direction, willing him not to catch me before I can find help. Before I can find my guardian angel.

CHAPTER TWO

Campbell

I wipe my hands off on my jeans as I watch the new foal stand on shaky legs and totter over to his mother. I rest my arms on the stall door, watching the new family as they nuzzle each other. My mare, Delilah, finally went into labor this afternoon and it's been a long few hours helping her deliver her foal. Both mom and son are here and healthy though now and it's time for me to make my way to bed. I need to be up early, as usual, to help my men take care of things around here.

I pat the stall door, taking one last look at them before I pick up a stray halter, hanging it on a hook outside another stall as I pass. I close up the barn and turn to head up to my house, stopping to stare into the woods and wonder about my girl as usual. I stop and listen closer. I could have sworn I heard a sound coming from the woods. I pause, my body turning towards where I thought the sound was coming from. I hear it again and this time it's closer. I take a step closer to the woods and that's when she runs out.

My princess. Salem.

I'm struck and my whole body freezes, eyes locked on the little girl as she spots me and starts to run right towards me. This can't be happening. I must be so sleep deprived that I'm starting to hallucinate things. I watch as Salem runs closer and I see the terrified look on her face. That snaps me out of it and I run towards her, eyes already scanning the trees behind her for the danger.

We reach each other and I open my arms. She runs right into them and I wrap my body around hers, trying to shield her from whatever she was running from.

"Don't let him get me." She whimpers into my chest.

"Who?" I ask, panicked eyes still scanning the trees.

"My father. Please. Please don't let him get me."

Having her wrapped around me, finally, feels like a dream but she's trembling, shaking in my arms and I need to get her inside, somewhere where I can protect her. I look down and notice her feet are muddy and dirty. My stomach drops at seeing my girl, my princess, like this. I look up into her face and see tears falling from her pale blue eyes. I reach up, brushing her tears away when I hear a branch snap close by. My princess's eyes widen and she tenses in my arms. I bend down and scoop her up into my arms, taking off for the house.

I make it to the porch and swing the door open, kicking it closed with my foot and turning to lock it. I peek out the window and I can see a dark figure standing by the trees, looking left and right. He's not going to find what he's looking for. I tighten my grip on my princess and look down at her in my arms.

"Salem?" I ask, still not believing that she's really here.

"Campbell." She says as she wraps her thin arms tighter around my neck.

She's smaller than I remember, maybe only 5'2" and one hundred pounds. She's still beautiful with a round face and long brown hair that's tangled around her face. Her hair is longer too, hanging down to her waist and I do my best to not tug on it as I carry her. I look down and see her small tits are practically visible in her thin shift dress. Her little nipples are pebbled and poking against the fabric.

I clear my throat as I look away and my eyes scan down as I take in the rest of her tiny scrap of a dress that barely covers her pussy. It's riding up now as she's cradled in my arm and is pooled around the tops of her thighs. I can just see the edges of her plain white panties and I can feel her bare thighs where I'm cradling her and my dick hardens in my jeans.

I look away quickly, not wanting to get carried away and scare my girl. My eyes continue down her legs over the mud-caked calves and down to her little toes. I can already see scratches on her knees and feet and I make my way towards the bathroom so that I can get her cleaned and bandaged up.

I make my way down the hallway and into my room. I carry Salem into the bathroom and set her on the little sink, stepping back and moving around the small space. I turn the bathwater on and check the temperature, making sure it's not too hot before I walk back over to her.

"We need to get you cleaned up so that I can take care of these cuts." I say.

She just nods before she wiggles around on the counter. I step forward-thinking that she needs help getting down but she surprises me by pulling her dress up and over. I jerk back and around so fast that I smack my head off the door frame. *Jesus Christ.* I rub my head as I stand facing away from the bathroom. I hear Salem step into the bathtub and I slowly turn back around.

My eyes land on her dirty dress and little white panties lying in a pile on the floor. I follow the trail of mud to the bathtub and swallow as I take in the angel sitting in it. I swallow as my eyes dart anywhere but at her. My cock is hungry to devour the sight of her wet naked body but I don't want her to feel uncomfortable around me. I rack my brain for something to say.

"Happy birthday." I whisper. Her eyes snap to mine, surprise widening them.

"You remembered?"

"I remember everything about you, Salem."

I want to tell her that I circle the date in every

calendar that I've ever had. I used to bring her little presents on her birthday and I still have the one I got her last year but was never able to give her. Her father had stopped her from seeing me by then. Her eyes look away from mine and down to the mud on the floor. *I wonder if I should grab the present now.*

"Sorry." She whispers and my eyes snap to hers.

"For what?"

"Putting you in this situation. The mess." She says looking to the floor. "I promise I'll clean it up before I leave."

"Leave?" Panic sets in when I think about my girl leaving me. I just got her back. I can't lose her again.

She blinks up at me with her mouth hanging open.

"I-"

She's interrupted by a knock at the door and her eyes widen. I put my finger to my mouth, motioning for her to be quiet. She nods and I make my way to the front door. Picking up Salem's duffle bag that must have fallen when we came in and setting it behind the door. I look out the window and see her father standing on my front porch.

I take a deep breath before I unlock the door and pull it open. I'm ready to stake my claim, to fight him for Salem if it's necessary. I glare at him as I swing the door open. There's no way this asshole is getting anywhere near my princess. Not while I'm around.

CHAPTER THREE

Salem

I wash off quickly in the bathtub, using Campbell's soap to clean off. I love having his scent on me. I drain the tub and wrap a towel around my body. I lean over the tub, trying my best to rinse out the dirt on the bottom before I grab a washcloth and start on the floor. I clean up as much of the dirt as I can. I'm still on my hands and knees when Campbell comes back into the bathroom.

"He's gone, princess." He says as I stand to my feet.

He's got my duffle bag in his hand and I walk over to him to take it. I pull out my favorite dress, pulling it on as I let the towel drop from my body. I hear Campbell's sharp inhale of breath and I tug the dress over my head, looking up at him to see him swallowing hard and looking down my body. My eyes follow his and I don't see anything out of the ordinary.

"What?" I ask, "What's wrong?"

"Nothing." He says, his eyes meeting mine.

I zip my duffle bag up before I hop up on the sink next to it. I look down at my knees and feet. The cuts aren't deep but I can see that they're starting to bleed again.

"I'll probably just need a few bandages." I say, looking back up at him.

His eyes are back to staring at my legs.

"Do you not like blood?" I ask. I try to rack my brain for him ever mentioning it when we were younger but come up empty. It's the only thing I can think of for why he keeps just staring wide-eyed at me though.

"Not on you." He says quietly.

"I can bandage myself up. I should get out of here soon before my father comes back." I say looking worriedly back towards the front door.

"I told him I hadn't seen you and to get off my property. He won't be coming back."

I look up at Campbell, trying to decide if that will really be enough to keep my father away. I can't risk getting caught and being forced to go back to live in that prison with him.

"Let me bandage you up, princess." He says as he drags a first aid kit out of a cabinet.

He sets it on the counter next to my hip, flipping the lid and digging through the kit. I watch his hands as they dig through the tubes and bandages, finally pulling out some Neosporin and band-aids. Campbell's hands look strong like I remember, with callouses on his fingers and palms. His hands

15

look rough, but they're gentle as they tend to my wounds. Old scars dot the back of his hands and wrists and I stare at them as he cleans me up.

As Campbell focuses on taking care of my cuts, I take his distraction to study him. He's much like I remember. Tall, at least a foot taller than me and wide. He's got more muscles than I've ever seen on anyone. His face is tanned and covered in a short beard which is new but I already love it on him. It makes him look even more like a man.

His eyes flick up to me and I take a moment to admire their color. He has blue eyes like me, but his are a dark navy blue with a cooper ring circling the pupil. We stare at each other for a minute and I watch as his thick tongue comes out and licks his full bottom lip. He leans into me and I hold my breath.

He's going to kiss me again. I wonder what his beard will feel like. Will it hurt? Or tickle?

I lean in closer to him and I can feel his warm breath as it fans over my face. I look up into his eyes and see them focused on my lips. I lean closer to him trying to leverage myself up on the counter even more. He steps between my legs and I spread my thighs wide to accommodate his size. I wrap my legs around his waist and hiss as his jeans brush against a cut on my foot. Campbell pulls back immediately and he has my foot in his hands a minute later.

"Sorry, princess. I got distracted. Let me finish taking care of you."

"It's ok. I liked you getting distracted." I admit shyly.

"Me too." He says under his breath.

His finger brushes along my foot and the feeling tickles. I giggle as I try to pull my foot away from him. Campbell smiles up at me, grabbing my ankle tightly and bringing my foot back to him. He tickles my foot for a minute and I giggle and squirm on the countertop. My legs spread open wider as my dress scrunches up around my hips. Campbell smiles at me before he sees how I'm spread out in front of him.

His eyes darken as they lock between my legs. I can feel the tingles start at my center and I let my legs fall open wider. Campbell has been the only one to ever make me feel like this. I used to get tingles between my legs when we were younger and he would hold my hand or kiss me but this feels different. Maybe because there isn't a fence separating us this time.

I know that I should cover up but I'm addicted to the way that Campbell is staring down at me. Campbell's hands come down on my knees and he snaps my legs closed. The weight of his hands on my knees and the pressure from him pushing my legs together only causes the tingles in my center to increase. I moan as I try to scoot closer to him on the counter.

"That feels good."

"Salem." Campbell groans as his hands trace higher up my thighs.

My hands grip onto his shoulders as I try to work my hips closer to him. I lift one hand up and trail it along his beard.

"I like this." I say as my fingers keep touching it. The wiry hairs tickle my palms and I smile as I rub it back and forth across my hands.

"It tickles." I say with a laugh as I continue to rub it across my palms. "Will it tickle me everywhere?" I ask as I look up at him.

He groans long and low as he screws his eyes shut tight. His hands tighten on my legs and my dress rides up higher. I can feel the cold counter on my bare bottom and I moan at the different sensations. Campbell is making me so hot and I can feel as my wetness drips out of me to pool on the vanity beneath me.

"Do you want to find out, princess?" He asks huskily.

I nod and Campbell drops to his knees in front of me. He pulls my hips all the way to the edge of the counter before he leans forward and I can feel his hot breath as he takes a deep breath of me. I feel the scratchy hairs of his beard next as he leans closer and then, his warm wet tongue as it parts my delicate flesh.

He takes long, slow licks up my center as I lean back on the sink. I've been fantasizing about Campbell touching me like this for years but this is better than anything I could have imagined. I moan as he eats at me, gasping when he licks a special spot between my legs. It feels like he plugged me into a socket and he licks and sucks at the same spot over and over. My hips rock against his face and I can feel the hairs of his beard as they scrape along my sensitive flesh. He licks and sucks my pussy until the tingles get too big and I can't hold them back anymore. I go off like a firework, collapsing back against the mirror and sink as he licks me until I come back down.

I close my eyes, trying to calm my heart and slow my breathing. I feel him as he stands and then lifts me into his arms. I rest my head against his shoulder and yawn as I feel him carry me out of the bathroom. My eyes get heavier and I close them, just for a minute, as he lays me down on a bed. I can smell Campbell's scent all around me and I start to drift off as he pulls a blanket over me.

"Sleep, princess." He whispers against my forehead.

CHAPTER FOUR

Campbell

I tuck Salem in before I head back into the bathroom. I hate to wash her scent off of me but I'm dirty from working the farm all day and I desperately need a shower. I take one last lick of my lips, trying to get the last of her taste from them before I strip off my clothes and turn the water on.

I crank the hot water and quickly step under the spray. I soap and rinse off quickly, tugging on some new boxers before I brush my teeth and step back into my bedroom. My house is a simple farmhouse, like most houses in this area. It's settled on the south side of my 200-acre farm. The house is a white one story with a black roof and black trim with a wrap-around porch.

There's another house a couple of yards away that my men bunk down in. The bunkhouse is set up in much the same way as my home is with a kitchen and bathroom. There are more rooms in the bunkhouse with bunk beds built into each one. All of my single workers live in the bunkhouse and the married ones live nearby or in town with their families.

Our barns are set up in a half-circle past the bunkhouse and past that is just corrals and fenced-in fields. My farm is the largest in town, providing milk and meat to most people in this area. The town isn't very big and I employ most of the people around here, or I have in the past. It's one of those places where everyone around here pretty much knows everyone else.

This house had belonged to my parents but they left it to me a couple of months ago, along with the farm, before they retired and headed south. They left it to me when they realized that I wasn't going to leave until I had the girl next door with me. I had put off parties and after school activities in high school because they would have interfered with our nightly walks. Then I had put off college because that would have brought me even further from her.

She keeps talking about her leaving but I can't let that happen. I've known since I first saw her that she is meant to be mine. I can't let her get away or leave me. I can't even imagine what would happen if her father found her again.

I head back into my bedroom and see Salem still curled up on her side. She's laying in the center of the bed with her damp hair fanned out across the pillow. I glance at the clock and see that it's after midnight. I have to be up in less than five hours and I already know that I'm going to be dragging tomorrow. I slip into bed beside Salem, pulling her into my arms and think about how she's worth a thousand sleepless nights.

I tuck her into me, practically dragging her on top of me so I'll feel if she tries to slip away without waking me. I wrap my arms around her waist and tug her higher on me so we're laying chest to chest. Our legs tangle together under the sheets and I love the feeling of her weight on top of me as we sleep. She's so small compared to me but having her wrapped in my arms makes me feel better. No one will be able to hurt her with me wrapped around her like this. Her head rests on my shoulder and I tuck her head under my chin, following her into sleep.

***

I wake the next morning with Salem still sprawled out across my chest. I smile to myself as I feel her wiggle on top of me, sighing as she gets comfortable. I never set an alarm, my body is too used to waking up with the sun and as I look over now, I see it's just before 4:30 am. I need to get up and start my day but I don't want to disturb or leave Salem. She's had a long night too and she needs her rest.

I reach over, grabbing my cellphone off the end table and send a quick message to my foreman,

Paul, letting him know that I'll be in late today. He sends back a thumbs up and I toss my cellphone down, wrapping Salem tighter in my arms. I used to imagine laying just like this in my head. We would fall asleep together every night just like this and wake up wrapped in each other's arms too. I lay there for a couple more hours, thinking that all of those fantasies are about to come true, as the sun starts to creep through the windows, shining over the princess sleeping on my chest.

I had tried to go back to sleep but I had to think of a way to get Salem to agree to stay. I had to find a way to protect her and keep her safe from her father or anyone else who wanted to take her from me. I came up with a pretty simple solution, one that I'm all for, but I'm not sure how Salem will take it.

She finally starts to stir at about 8 am and I lay still while she squirms and stretches on top of me. She pushes up and I can barely see her face through all of her hair. I laugh as I reach up and push the long locks out of the way.

"There you are, princess." I tease.

She smiles brightly down at me and before I know it, her mouth is on mine. Her lips are the same as I remember from our one and only kiss. Her tongue licks against mine and I open under her, letting her slip her tongue into my mouth. She slides her tongue against mine and moans as she feels my beard against her face. Her hands come up and once again slip into my beard. She pulls back, giggling as she runs her hands across it.

"You like my beard, huh?"

"Oh yeah." She says with a smile.

"I was going to shave it today, I only let it grow out because we were so busy around here."

"NO! Please don't Campbell."

Yeah, like I'm ever getting rid of this thing now. I love the way she can't seem to keep her hands off it way too much.

"Don't worry, princess. I'm keeping it. I'll keep it for as long as you want."

"Good." She says before she brings her mouth back to mine.

We lay there in bed kissing for a while and it's already the best day of my life. She slides her hands into my hair, tugging on the long strands and I bring my hands into her hair too. I wrap the long locks around my fingers, using her hair to tug her head back so I can lick and kiss down her neck. She grinds her hips down into mine as I nip at her collarbone, sucking gently on her sensitive skin.

I bring one hand down to her hip, helping to control her movements as she rocks on top of me. I can feel my erection pulse as it stretches the front of my boxers. She wiggles up and down the length as I continue to explore her neck. She's naked underneath her dress and I can feel her damp folds as they slip up and down my length.

I grit my teeth, trying not to come in my underwear like a thirteen-year-old when there's a knock at the front door. I growl into Salem's neck as she stills and tenses on top of me.

"Do you think it's my father again?" She asks with a slight tremor in her voice.

"I'll take care of it if it is, Princess."

I drag myself from the bed, slipping on a pair of gym shorts as I will my erection to go down. I shuffle out to the front door and see my foreman, Paul, standing there. I unlock the door, swinging it open.

"What's up?"

"There's something wrong with Delilah. I've already called the vet but I didn't know if there was anything I should know about last night or her labor."

"No, labor went smooth and her and the foal were fine when I left." I say frowning.

"Ok, well, vet should be here soon. I'll let you know what he says."

I thank Paul and tell him I'll see him in a little bit before heading back inside.

"It wasn't your dad, princess. There's something wrong with one of the horses. She gave birth last night and isn't doing too well this morning."

"Oh no." Salem say and I can see the concern in her eyes.

"I'm going to go check on her real quick before the vet gets here but there's something else I wanted to talk to you about." I say slowly.

"What's that?" She asks, turning to me with big pale blue eyes.

"Will you marry me."

CHAPTER FIVE

Salem

Marry him?

"Yes!" I say, throwing myself into his arms.

I can't believe that this is happening. It feels like all of my dreams are coming true. Campbell is all I've ever wanted and I can't wait to be his wife. Then I realize why he's probably doing this. Campbell has always been sweet and generous and he's more protective of me than most. My fingers start to nervously pull at my hair, quickly braiding it to the side. Campbells fingers come up to my chin, pushing my face up until my eyes meet his.

"Are you just asking me to marry you so my father can't get me?" I ask.

"No, of course not. I love you, Salem. I have since the day that we met. I would do anything for you, would do anything to keep you safe from your father, but I also want to marry you. I desperately want you to be my wife."

"Ok." I say. "Then yes, I'll marry you."

He smiles down at me and I feel my own lips curve up at the sight.

"We'll head to the courthouse this morning then, princess. Why don't you go ahead and get ready while I check out Delilah?"

I nod and he leans down, dropping a sweet kiss on my lips. I smile as he turns and walks out of the bedroom. I grab my duffle bag and head into the bathroom. *I wonder if I have anything white.* I start tugging out clothes until I finally find a white dress and my only pair of dress shoes I only had two pairs of shoes and I lost one in the mud puddle on my run here. The dress shoes aren't broken in and I know they'll kill my feet but I don't have any other options. The dress I pick out is another shift, white this time with a shiny sheen to it.

I decide to take a quick shower before I get dressed. I use Campbell's soap again and smile as I wrap a fluffy towel around my body. I drag his comb through my hair, getting rid of any tangles before I braid it to the side. I use Campbell's toothbrush and toothpaste and then step back to check my appearance. I don't have any makeup or anything so this will have to do.

I grab my dress and tug it on over my head, making sure the spaghetti straps are firmly in place. I grab a new pair of panties next and I'm sliding them up my legs when Campbell comes back into the room. He stops and stares at me with his mouth hanging open.

"Do you like it?" I ask, spinning around so that

he can see all of it. The skirt on the dress flies up around my waist.

Campbells next to me in an instant. His hands wrap around my waist, tugging the short dress back into place. He's frowning down at the hem and I look to see if there's a stain or tear.

"You don't like it?" I ask.

"I love it, princess, but let's not spin around in public. Can't have you showing others what's mine."

"What's yours?"

"This." He says his hand slipping around to my front and cupping my pussy.

His fingers smooth back and forth over the fabric of my panties and my legs widen as I let out a moan. He continues to tease me over the fabric of my panties and the tingles are starting to come back. My head falls back as his finger sneaks under my panties and then his bare skin is there on mine. He starts to tease around my hole and my hips start to rock in time with his movements.

"You're so wet, Salem."

I moan as my eyes try to focus on his. His fingers continue to tease my wet flesh and my hands come up, gripping his shoulders to try to steady myself. My body is starting to tense and the tingles are getting stronger.

"That's it, princess. Come for me."

I don't know if it's his words or his fingers but my body does as he commands, my cream flooding out to cover his fingers. Campbell keeps stroking me as my body turns to jelly in his arms. He holds me up with the hand around my back and slips the other one out from under my dress. I watch as he brings his fingers to his mouth, licking them clean.

I pant as he stares down at me. He gives me a smile before he leans down and kisses me. I can taste my release on his lips and I moan at the flavor. His beard scrapes against my face, reminding me of when he went down on me last night. I kiss him harder and his arms wrap around me tighter in response. He pulls back after a minute.

"Come on, princess. I made us some food. Let's eat or it will be cold."

He twines his fingers with mine and tugs me after him down the hallway and into a cozy kitchen. His whole house is cozy and seems well-loved. Everything is clean and taken care of and I'm struck by how different it is from my father's house.

He leads me into the kitchen before pulling out a chair for me at the kitchen table. He's already got two place settings ready with some eggs and toast on each. I settle into my chair and start to dig in. He's a good cook and I finish the food quickly.

"Did you want more?" He asks once I've cleaned my plate.

"No, that was perfect. Thank you."

"Let me get changed and then we can head to the courthouse." I watch him head back to the bedroom and I bring the dishes over to the sink, quickly washing them and leaving them in the rack to dry. I guess I'll have to figure out where everything goes around here soon if I'm going to be living here.

I hear Campbell's footsteps behind me and I turn around to see him in a pair of dark wash jeans with a white button-up shirt. He has a pair of worn dark boots on and he does a spin for me. I giggle as he turns back to me and he smiles before grabbing my hand and leading me out to a nice black truck. His hands grip my hips and he lifts me into the cab.

He points out different sites on the twenty-minute drive into town and I stare around at the unfamiliar views. I look around with wide eyes for the whole drive and eventually, Campbell pulls up outside of a nice white building.

"Let me get your door." He says as he jumps up and runs around to the passenger side.

I let him lift me down and he closes the door before he grips my hand and leads me up the stairs to the front doors. He leads me inside and we walk up to a long desk where a little old lady is sorting through some papers. She looks up at us as we approach, giving us a warm smile.

"Morning, Campbell! What can I do for you two?" She asks sweetly.

"We'd like to get married." Campbell says.

She looks a little startled but congratulates us as she gathers some papers for us to fill out. We sign the forms before we hand everything back to her and then she points us around the corner to another room. I follow Campbell inside and see a judge standing there. He shakes our hands and then the ceremony starts. It's over in a matter of minutes and we walk back out to his truck as man and wife.

"We'll have to stop and get rings." He says as he lifts me into the truck.

I buckle up and he starts the truck. I think he's going to head home but he starts going in the opposite direction.

"Where are we going?" I ask.

"To get rings. We'll have to go to the next town since there's nowhere here to get that kind of thing."

"Oh." I say as I sit back in my seat. It's weird having lived here my whole life but not really knowing anything about the place.

"What are you thinking about, princess?"

"How weird it is that I don't know anything about this place. It's supposed to be my home, right? But it's so foreign to me. My father never let me leave our property. He would make me stay inside and I was never allowed to leave the yard. I used to beg with him to let me go with him to town but he never let me."

I see Campbell's fingers tighten on the steering wheel and my finger tangle in the hem of my dress. We're silent for a little bit before Campbell reaches over and slips his fingers between mine.

"I won't be the same as him. I love you and I won't keep you locked up like he did. I'll take you anywhere you want to go, Salem. Just say the word and we'll leave. You can do whatever you want, ok princess?"

I nod as I feel tears threaten to spill over at his sweet words. Campbell has always been so perfect.

I never had to worry that I would be trapped with him like I was with my father. We're silent for the rest of the trip but every now and then his fingers squeeze around mine.

CHAPTER SIX

Campbell

We go to a fancy looking jewelry shop and spend about an hour looking at rings. I know that I just want a plain silver band but Salem has a hard time deciding. I stand next to her patiently as she looks at tray after tray. Finally, I see her eyes light up and know that she's found the one.

It's a heart-shaped diamond in a platinum setting and she picks out another band with tiny diamonds laid in for her wedding band. We luck out and they have the ring in her size. We opt to wear it out of the store and I quickly hand over my card, signing the slip before I pick up her hand in mine and lead her out of the store.

We walk out and I look over to see Salem holding her hand out, twisting her fingers so the light shines off the ring.

"It's so pretty!" She says, hopping lightly.

Her dress jumps up with her movements and

I tug her closer into my side. I look around and see a few other guys staring at my girl and licking their lips. I glare at them until they turn away before I help my princess into the truck. I hop behind the wheel and she shifts in her seat so she's facing me. Her shiny dress slips higher on her thighs and I shift in my seat, trying to hide my growing bulge.

"Are you happy, princess?" I ask.

She looks away from her ring to beam at me.

"Yeah, I am. I love you, Campbell."

I smile back at her before I start the truck up.

"Are you hungry? There's more places to eat here than if we head back to our town."

"I could eat." She says as her stomach growls

I laugh at her reaction.

"What are you hungry for?"

"Hmm, Tacos!" She says excitedly as she sees a sign for a little restaurant up ahead.

I steer the car into the parking lot and lead Salem into the restaurant. We seat ourselves and the waitress comes over to get our order. We both order some tacos and nachos with water. We spend the rest of our lunch talking. I ask her about the year that we didn't see each other and tell her about my parents buying a home in Florida and moving a couple of months ago.

We finish lunch and make the drive back home. I look over at her as we get closer and see her frowning as she stares out the window.

"What's wrong, princess?"

"Nothing."

"Come on." I say as I nudge her with my elbow.

"It's just, this feels like some kind of dream, like I'm going to wake up at any moment and be back in that house. You'll be gone and I'll be alone again."

"I'm not going anywhere, Salem. We're married now. That means until death do us part. I won't let him take you from me. I won't let anyone take you from me. I promise, princess."

This seems to help calm her and she settles back in her seat. I hold her hand for the rest of the trip. We've been gone most of the day and I know that I'll need to head out to the barn to check things out and make sure that everything is ok. I pull down the long driveway and park outside the house. I help Salem down and unlock the door. She plops down on the couch and I want to join her so badly but I know I need to go check on things first.

"I need to head out and make sure everything is alright. I'll only be gone a little bit. Did you want to come with me?"

"These shoes are killing my feet. Is it ok if I just stay here?"

"Of course, princess. I won't be gone long anyways. Stay here and relax."

I kiss her forehead before I head out the back-door and jog out to the barn. I walk in and everything looks in its place. I run into my foreman, Paul, and he tells me what they did today. Paul tells me about a calf that we might need to keep an eye on and how the new foal is doing. The vet left and said that Delilah was just a little dehydrated. We'll have to keep an eye on her.

I thank Paul for running things today and he tells me congratulations. I smile back at him. I should have known that word of our marriage would have already spread. Everything seems to be running smoothly on the farm so I tell him I'll see him tomorrow before I head back to the house. I hear raised voices as I get closer and I immediately start to run towards the house.

I round the corner and see Salem standing there with her father. He looks pissed, his face red and frozen into a murderous scowl. He's got his hand wrapped tight around Salem's upper arm as he tries to drag her out of the house. Her eyes meet mine and I can see the terror and pain written on her face then. She is terrified of him and my blood starts to boil as he pulls her out of the house.

I sprint towards them, getting to them in seconds and ripping his hand off of my princess.

"Get your hands off my wife." I snarl and his eyes flare as they turn to me.

"She is my daughter. She did not have my permission to marry you. I'm taking her home. Not get out of our way." He shouts back.

"She's eighteen, she doesn't need your permission. We were married this morning. Salem is my wife now. She's not going anywhere with you, now, get off of our property before I call the cops."

Her father glares at me and looks back towards his daughter.

"This is what you want? To stay here with this-this stranger?" He sputters.

"Campbell isn't a stranger. He's my husband." Salem says with a proud lift to her chin.

"You stupid, naïve, brat. He's going to use you and throw you away. Your mother would have-"

I cut him off as he tries to continue to berate my girl.

"Get. Off. Our. Property."

I take a step towards him and he backs down quickly. Turning and heading back to his truck. He glares over his shoulder once more before climbing behind the wheel and peeling out of our driveway. I sigh as I watch him leave before I turn back to Salem.

CHAPTER SEVEN

Salem

I stand next to Campbell as we silently watch my father speed away. When I had first heard the knock on the front door, I had just assumed that Campbell or one of his men needed something. Then I opened the door to see my father standing there, breathing hard and looking furious. My heart had started beating so hard that I could hear it in my ears and I was so afraid that he was going to make me go home with him.

He had called me a stupid girl, a whore, and worse and tried to drag me out of the house. I don't know what I would have done if Campbell hadn't come around the corner and saved me. He really is my guardian angel.

My mind flashes back to what my father said about Campbell. He's wrong. Campbell isn't a stranger. I know him better than I know anyone and I know he feels the same way about me. I know it seems like we're too young or we moved too fast but that's not how it feels. I've loved Campbell since we were kids and I know he feels the same way. Just because we haven't seen each other in the last year doesn't mean that our feelings for each other have changed.

Campbell has been nothing but nice to me. He's tried to take care of me and protect me since we met. He loves me and I love him. We're married now and I know that we each took our vows seriously.

We watch my father leave in silence before Campbell turns and escorts me into the house. I'm silent while we make our way back inside and Campbell steers me over to the kitchen table. He leaves me there while he goes over to the stove and I watch as he makes some tea and sandwiches. I'm not really hungry but I don't have the heart to tell him that. He carries everything over to the table and I take a drink of the tea before I pick at the sandwich.

This isn't how I pictured spending my wedding night but my father's arrival seems to have pushed us off track and destroyed any mood that was there.

"Are you ok, princess?" Campbell asks, snapping me out of my thoughts.

"Yeah, seeing him just threw me."

"I'll never let him take you back there. You're mine now. I love you, Salem."

"I love you, too. I know that you would never let anyone hurt me. I don't even think that he would hurt me, I just don't want to go back there and be trapped again."

"You won't. You won't ever be trapped again." He says as he picks up one of my hands.

I smile at him as I take another sip of my tea. We're silent for a minute before Campbell speaks again.

"Will you tell me about the last year? Why doesn't he want you to leave?"

I can feel my shoulders tense but I know I need to let him in. He's my husband now after all and he loves me.

"I think that he was afraid of something happening to me too. It was just the two of us after my mom died in labor and I think that he just lost it when she died. Or maybe he was always like this? I don't know. It's hard to picture him being any other way. He could be so cruel. Sometimes my dad used to get drunk and tell me that I killed her, I killed my mom."

"Salem, you have to know that that's not true." Campbell says squeezing my hand tight.

"I do, I do." I assure him. "He would home-school me and that took up most of the day and then he would kind of just let me be by myself. It wasn't all bad though. I love to read, you know, and he would let me go outside every day, it's just... I was so alone. I missed seeing you every day. I missed you so much, Campbell." I say and I can feel the tears starting to fall.

"I missed you too, Princess."

He picks me out of my chair then and cradles me in his lap. I cry into his shirt as I remember how alone and sad, I was the last year. How alone I really was even before then.

"I can give you the friends, take you into town and introduce you to everyone I know." He offers, already trying to find a solution, to make me happy.

I nod against him as I lay in his arms. We stay like that until our tea grows cold and my father fades from my head. I shift in his arms and his beard tickles my forehead. I remember what he did to me this morning and last night, how his beard scratched softly against my thighs and I remember that tonight is our wedding night. We shouldn't let my father ruin that for us.

"Campbell?"

"Hmm?"

"Take me to bed."

CHAPTER EIGHT

Campbell

My body tenses at her words. I would love nothing more than to take Salem to bed and claim her but I need to make sure that she's all right, emotionally, before we do anything.

"Are you sure, Salem? We don't have to do anything tonight. I've waited years for you, I can wait longer if you need me too."

"I don't want to wait any longer. I love you, Campbell. I want you to make love to me."

I look down into her pleading eyes and know there's no way that I can deny her. I've waited so long to have her under me.

"I love you too, Salem. I'm going to be so good for you, so good to you. I won't let anyone hurt you and I promise I'll make sure that you get whatever you want."

She kisses me then and I scoop her up in my arms, carrying her down the hallway and into our bedroom. I should have done something romantic, like flowers or candles but I don't have any of that stuff here. I look down at Salem though and she's just staring up at me. I realize that she doesn't care about that stuff; she just wants me.

I lay her down in the middle of the bed before I lay down on top of her. I keep most of my weight on my elbows, not wanting to crush her. I cup her face in my hands as our mouths meet and as the kiss deepens, I move my hands up, tangling them in her long hair.

She moans into my mouth and her legs come up, wrapping around the back of my thighs. I should have taken my jeans off, I realize. She starts to rock against my hard length through the denim and I've never seen anything sexier in my life. I start to circle my hips, rubbing her on my hard bulge as our lips meet again and again.

Our tongues tangle, our kisses sloppy. Both of us are inexperienced. I met Salem when I was ten and as soon as I saw her, I knew that she was it for me. There's never been anyone but her and there never will be.

Her tiny hands start to push at my shoulders and I push up on my hands, thinking I must have been too heavy on top of her. I open my mouth to apologize when her fingers start to undo the buttons on my shirt.

"Take it off, Campbell. I want to feel you against me."

I swear I almost come in my jeans but I lean back and do as she asks. I stare down at her while

I slip my shirt off. Her shiny dress is bunched up around her belly button and both of the straps have been tugged or fallen down her shoulders. She looks like every wet dream that I've ever had and I have to bite back a groan when her hands go to my waist and she starts to undo my jeans.

I let her unbutton them and tug the zipper down before I move off the bed and push my jeans and boxers off. I stand back up and look at her but her eyes are locked on my dick. It's hard and pointing straight up, the red head almost reaching my belly button. I reach down, giving it a few strokes while she watches. A drop of precum slips out and I watch as she sits up fully and licks her lips.

"Can I taste you?" She asks shyly.

"Fuck, princess." I say as my hand tightens around my length.

"You got to taste me." She pleads.

"Salem, if you wrap your lips around me right now, I will come. Immediately." I stress.

"I want to taste you, Campbell."

God, she's got me so wrapped around her finger. I can't deny her and I slowly step towards the bed as she kneels in the center. She reaches down and pulls her thin dress over her head, kneeling before me in just a pair of white cotton panties.

I can't take it and before she can even touch me, I'm coming. Thick white streams pump out of me to land on the bedspread and the carpet by my feet. My head tips back and I close my eyes as I try to catch my breath. My hand is still wrapped around my cock when suddenly, I feel something flick against my fingers. I jerk, looking down to see Salem on her knees before me, her little pink tongue licking up my mess. My cock jerks to life again and I groan as she starts to lick up my length.

She continues to lick and suck along my length until I'm hard and pulsing. I look down at her, my hands tangling in her hair to help hold it back from her face. She opens her mouth and her tongue takes its first lick on the tip of my cock. We both moan and the next thing I know, she's opened her mouth wider and taken half my length into her mouth. My knees grow weak and I have to force my hands from tightening even further in her hair.

She bobs her head up and down my length, sucking as she goes. I've never gotten a blow job before, only wanting to do these things with Salem, but already, I'm seeing what the hype is all about. This feels incredible. Better than I could have ever imagined. I'm close again but I don't want to come in her mouth. Besides, I think its far past time that I had my mouth back between her legs.

I tilt her head back, stepping away from her as she looks up at me.

"Your turn, princess." I say as I lift her off the ground.

I lay her back down in the center of the bed. She still has her white panties on and I can see they're soaked through. I can see her sex through the sheer material and lick my lips, already anticipating burying my face against that wet flesh. She spreads her legs wider and I take that as my cue, crawling up the bed and between her legs. I push her knees wider, settling my shoulders between her thighs.

"I love you, Salem." I whisper as I breathe her in.

"I love you too, Campbell." She says back as she tangles her fingers in my hair.

I rub my beard back and forth across the inside of her thighs and she moans at the feeling. I love that I can make her feel so good and I kiss the inside of her thigh before I reach up and slip her panties down her legs. I toss them over my shoulder before I lean back down and spread her lips. Her center is so wet and pink and I can't hold back any longer.

I start slow, giving her long licks up her center and swirling around her hard button. Her hips start to rock against my face and her moans get louder and louder. At her obvious pleasure, I start to pick up my pace, eating at her with a hunger I've never felt before. I lick her up the center one last time before I suck her little nub into my mouth, flicking it with my tongue.

She comes undone then and her whole body tenses as she shouts my name into the dark room. I rub my face against her sex one last time wanting as much of her passion on my face as possible. She twitches against me and I pull back, kissing my way up her body.

I stop at her small tits, rolling her nipple between my thumb and forefinger while I take the other one in my mouth. I tease her nipples, making sure to rub my beard against the sensitive peaks. I pull back and admire her rosy skin as I slide up her body.

She grins up at me before she leans up, molding her lips to mine. We fall back on the bed together and my thick erection lines up with her wet flesh. I pull away, needing to check one last time.

"Are you sure?" I ask.

"Absolutely."

I kiss her again as I start to slowly rock my hips against hers. My dick slowly pushes into her until I feel her barrier. I've been dreading this part. The thought of hurting my princess makes me sick but I know there's no way around this.

"I'm sorry, Salem. It will just hurt for a minute. Let me know if it's too much though and we'll stop. Ok? I promise we'll stop."

She nods up at me, her eyes wide and her fingers digging into my biceps. I kiss her again as I push through her virginity and seat myself fully inside of her. She tenses under me and I hold myself still, waiting for the go-ahead from her.

She pants under me and I lean down, sucking her tits back into my mouth. I nip and suck her tight peaks until her hips start to rock against mine.

"Campbell...move." Salem pants in my ear.

I slide my hips back, pulling almost all the way out before I pause and push back in. Feeling her silky heat wrapped around me is the single best feeling of my life. I swear my eyes roll back in my head as

I sink back into her.

We start a slow and steady pace until Salem starts to whine into my ear, begging me to go faster. Sweat coats our bodies, helping us glide together and I start to pick up my pace more as a tightening starts at the base of my spine. I know I don't have long before I come and I need to make sure that Salem finishes before I do.

I bring my fingers between us as I balance on my other arm. I find her clit and rub my fingers in circles over it, pushing down slightly. She screams my name at the first feeling of my fingers on her sensitive nub and when I pinch it between my fingers, she explodes.

She screams my name over and over again as her orgasm flows through her. Seeing her go off under me and hearing her scream my name has my orgasm bearing down on me. Her pussy tightens and pulses around my hard length and I can feel myself tense more as her pussy massages the come out of me.

I come with a shout as I erupt inside of her, shooting load after load of hot come into her waiting warmth. My arms give out and I almost collapse on top of her but I roll us at the last second. Our chests rise and fall together as we both try to catch our breaths. The sweat cools on our bodies as we both finally calm down. I stroke Salem's hair as her breathing evens out and before long we both fall asleep.

CHAPTER NINE

Salem

My eyes blink open and I realize that I'm sprawled out on top of Campbell. I cross my arms over his chest and rest my head on top of my hands, staring down at my sleeping husband's face. So much has happened in the last 24 hours and I realize that I haven't really taken the time to stop and just appreciate the man under me.

Last night was incredible. It was better than I ever imagined in any of my fantasies, and that's saying something because I fantasized about making love with Campbell a lot. I've never felt so connected to someone before and when he came before I even touched him, well I had never felt sexier or more wanted in my life.

My hair falls around my face and I push it back. Campbell starts to stir under me and I smile down at him as he blinks sleepily up at me. As soon as the sleep clears from his eyes, he smiles up at me and I lean down and kiss him. He moans against my lips before he opens under me and slips his tongue in my mouth.

I shift on top of him and feel his hard length against my thigh. He's already ready for me and I shift more, lining him up with my opening. I push back onto him and slowly take him inside of me. He groans against my neck as I sink fully onto him. It feels so much fuller when I take him like this and I sit up as I start to slowly rock my hips back and forth. I moan when his cock strokes over something inside of me and I bear down, making sure that he rocks against that spot again and again. I throw my head back and my hair pools on top of his thighs as I start to ride him harder, faster.

This time is different from last night and I can feel my orgasm pulsing under the surface already. I rest my hands on his chest as I lean over him. I look down to see him staring up at me with his mouth open. Seeing the lust written in every one of his features is too much and my nails dig into his chest as I come on his cock. His hands grip my hips as I pant on top of him and he moves me up and down his length, once, twice, before he groans and I feel him come deep inside me.

I collapse on top of him then and my long hair falls around us both. Campbell laughs as he gently pushes it back.

"Good morning, princess."

"Morning." I say, grinning at him.

"What time is it?" He asks as I roll off of him.

"Um, 5:15 am." I say as I look at the bedside clock.

Campbell groans as he stretches in bed. He rolls out on the other side and pads over to me. My eyes hungrily devour him as he makes his way over to me.

"Shower with me?" He asks.

I nod and he takes my hand as he leads me into the shower. I wait while he adjusts the water temperature before we both step under the spray. He washes me and I turn and wash him too. We rinse off and I wince when I turn a certain way. He's there immediately, his arms circling me.

"Are you ok? What's wrong?" He asks, concern and worry coloring his tone.

"I'm ok. Just a little sore." I say as the twinge passes.

Campbell smiles down at me lovingly. "We'll have to take it easy for a couple of days."

I pout up at him as he shuts the water off and wraps me in a towel. I let him dry me off and watch as he wraps a towel around his waist. We both head into the bedroom and I tug a short sleeve dress over my head. It falls around my thighs and I walk over to him as he pulls on his jeans. I kiss his cheek.

"I'll go make us some breakfast." I say as I head down the hall to the kitchen.

I clean up the dishes from last night as the eggs and toast cook. Campbell comes into the kitchen as I try to find the stuff to make coffee. He helps show me where everything is and tells me that I can rearrange anything that I want. I smile at him as I plate the eggs and he butters the toast. We carry everything over to the little kitchen table and I smile when he digs in.

"We should plan a honeymoon." He says as he finishes his food.

My ears perk up at the idea of getting to leave and see a new place.

"Really?" I ask excitedly.

"Of course. Anywhere you want to go. Why don't you use the computer today and look up some places and we can decide at lunch? Or did you want to come out to the barn with me today?"

We both look down to my short dress and I laugh.

"I think I'll stay here."

He smiles at me. "Why don't you order some more clothes too? I'll leave you my credit card and you can get whatever you want."

We clear the dishes and I set them in the sink, turning to find him standing behind me. He wraps his arms around me and I lean into him. My hands go into his beard and he grins down at me. I stand on my tiptoes and he bends down, his lips finding mine.

He pulls back before we can get too heated and I moan at the loss. He gives me a quick peck on the lips before he kisses my nose and then my forehead. I giggle at the feeling of his beard against my sensitive skin and he smiles down at me.

"I love you, Salem. So much."

I open my mouth to tell him that I love him

when colorful lights start to play across the wall above our heads. We both look out the front window as the police car comes down the driveway.

Not again, I think as I see my father's truck come barreling down the driveway next. Fear grips me that the cops are here. Could my father have done something? Is there some law that says that I have to go back and live in that house with him? Even though I'm married to Campbell now. I can feel my breath come in short pants as I get worked up and Campbell wraps his arms around me as we make our way outside to see what they want.

CHAPTER TEN

Campbell

I stand from my chair and wrap my arm around Salem's waist as we walk over to the door. I look out to see a cop car pulling up in front of the house. The cops get out and I sigh as they make their way towards the front door. I already know that this is Salem's father again. He must have called the cops when I wouldn't let him take her last night. I'm already thinking that we're going to have to get a restraining order against him.

"Why don't you stay inside while I sort this out?" I ask.

Salem's fingers are clenched in my shirt but she nods. I kiss her forehead before I open the door and meet the cop before he can step up to the door.

"Morning, Campbell." Sherriff Shephard says as he stops at the bottom of the steps.

"Sherriff Shephard, what can I do for you?" I ask.

"Is a Salem Mitchell here?"

"She is. It's Salem McConnely now."

"I heard. Congratulations." He says with a faint smile. "I still need to see her though. Mr. Mitchell here says that you're holding his daughter here against her will."

I glare at her father and he glares right back before turning back to the cops.

"His daughter and I are married. I married Salem yesterday morning and we both already told Mr. Mitchell that yesterday afternoon. He spoke to her and saw that she was fine. I'm not holding her against her will."

"Is that true, Mr. Mitchell? Did you see your daughter yesterday?" Shephard asks.

Both he and the other cop are inching their way closer to Salem's father as he starts pacing. I can see from his face and movements that he's becoming more and more agitated. He has to know that he's not going to get Salem back though.

"She just ran off and married him yesterday!" He yells. "She is my daughter and we've never even met this man before! She can't just marry some stranger! She is a young girl and she belongs at home with her father! She needs to come home with me NOW!" He demands.

"We have met before. I used to spend every evening with her until you stopped us a year ago! She is eighteen, an adult and she legally married me of her own free will. She is my wife now and she will stay here with me." I yell back.

I'm trying to rein my temper in but the thought of my princess having to go back to live with this man has me panicking.

"That's enough, both of you!" Sherriff Shephard yells.

He waits until we both take a deep breath before continuing.

"Seeing as your daughter is married to Mr. McConnely, we legally can't force her to go home. If she wants to stay here then she can."

"She doesn't want to stay here! She wants to come home!" He yells, getting worked up again.

"No, I don't."

We all turn to see Salem standing in the open doorway. I thought she would look scared but all I can see on her face is sadness.

"I want to stay here." She says as she steps closer to me, interlacing her fingers with mine. "With my husband."

I smile down at her before we both turn and look back at the cops.

"Then there's nothing for us to do here. Mr. Mitchell, you'll have to vacate the property. Let the newlyweds have some time together."

Salem's father is screaming and sputtering, face red as the Sherriff and Deputy drag him back to his car. They usher him in and then wait for him to leave before getting in their police cruiser. Her father peels out of the driveway like before and I wonder when we'll see him again.

I grip Salem's hand tighter in mine and once again

lead her back inside.

She follows after me and I turn and lock the door before leading her back into the kitchen. I'm not sure how she's going to react to this new visit but I shouldn't worry. My girl is strong and when I look at her, I see that she's not scared anymore. Instead, she just looks sad.

"You alright, princess?"

"Yeah. It's just hard to see him like that. There's never been a lot of love between us but it's still sad to picture him in that awful house all alone."

"It'll be ok." I say as I wrap her up in my arms.

I end up calling Paul and telling him I won't be out again today and he tells me he's got it covered. Salem and I cuddle up on the couch with my laptop in our laps. We spend the rest of the morning looking up places to visit and narrowing down where we want to go. We laugh as we argue about whether we should go to a beach or somewhere colder, somewhere remote or a tourist attraction.

We make soup and grilled cheese for lunch and cuddle back up on the couch to watch a movie. We're about halfway through the second movie when someone knocks on the front door. I slip out from under the blanket and make my way to the front door. When I see that it's Sherriff Shephard, I want to scream. We have to do something. I can't just keep letting Salem's father ruin our days together.

"Sheriff." I say as I step outside.

"Campbell. Is Salem here?"

"Of course she is. Where else would she be?"

"I need to speak with her."

"Why?"

"I'm afraid I have some bad news, son." He says and my stomach drops at those words.

I hear the door open behind me and Salem walks out to stand next to me. I wrap her in my arms and we stand like that while the sheriff tells us what happened. Salem stares wide-eyed at him as he tells her how her father was drunk and drove his car into a tree just a mile up the road.

"He must have left here and started drinking. We got the call about an hour ago that there had been a wreck. By the time we got there, he was gone. I'm so sorry for your loss, dear."

The sheriff holds his hat and we both stare down at Salem but she seems frozen. Finally, she just nods her head and looks up at me. I can see the sadness and guilt swirling in her eyes and I pull her closer into me. I whisper into her ear that it will be ok, over and over as I rock her back and forth. The sheriff leaves after he tells us that he'll be in contact with any other questions.

We can go down to the coroners tomorrow for the body and plan the funeral after that. My heart breaks for her. I hated the man and I wouldn't shed a tear for the bastard, not after how he treated my girl but my princess has a big heart and I know she wouldn't wish this on him, on anyone. That some part of her was hoping he would just leave us alone and we could all live happily.

I carry her into the house and lay her down in our bed. I slide in after her and spoon her as she cries herself to sleep.

CHAPTER ELEVEN

Salem

The funeral was yesterday and Campbell and I were the only ones to show. Campbell had held me while the priest said a few words. We had stood silent while they lowered the casket into the ground and then he had led me back to his truck.

The last four days have passed in a blur of funeral planning and grief. I still can't believe that my father is dead. I felt shock and sadness when the sheriff first told us the news but then the guilt and anger had set in. I was angry because he had treated me like a prisoner for years and I finally got away from him. I didn't owe him anything. Then the guilt would hit. Guilt that I hadn't just gone with him, then maybe he would still be alive, but I felt even more guilty that I wasn't really all that sad that he was dead.

I know he was my father and I feel like I should have loved him or cared for him but the truth is that he treated me like crap for too long and any affectionate feelings I might have had were used up long ago. I wish that we could have had a better relationship. I wish that I would have understood him or that he would have tried to understand me but it's too late for that now.

Campbell has been by my side through all of this. He's my rock and I don't know what I would have done if he wasn't here. He held my hand while we went to claim my father's body. He helped me decide on a casket and headstone and funeral plot and then he paid for all of it.

Today, he's helping me again.

We went back to my father's house. I inherited it and the land and we need to figure out what we want to do with it. I already know that the house will need to be torn down; it's in bad shape. Campbell drove me out here right after breakfast and we've been sitting in the truck for the last ten minutes. I've been trying to work up the courage to walk back into that house and Campbell has been sitting patiently with me.

Finally, I nod and throw my car door open. We both step down and start to make our way up the steps. I have to stop and point out to Campbell where the weak spots are and where he shouldn't step as we go but we eventually tiptoe our way inside. It's only been a week but it feels like I've been gone much longer than that.

"We can take anything you want to with us. Just let me know and I'll carry anything you want out to the truck. Ok, princess?"

I nod but I already know that I won't be taking anything with me. I tell Campbell to stay on the first floor. The stairs are falling apart and there's no way that they would be able to hold up under his weight. I pick my way upstairs and look around but almost everything was moved downstairs so it's pretty bare.

I walk back towards the stairs and see Campbell waiting for me at the bottom. He wasn't happy about me going up the stairs, said they were too dangerous and I can see the worry still there as I start to make my way down them. He holds his hand out to me as soon as I'm within reach and helps me down the last few stairs.

"Nothing upstairs?"

"No, it's empty. We had brought everything down when the stairs got bad."

He follows after me as I go into the living room and then the kitchen, asking me if I want any of the furniture or dishes. Everything is so old though that it should just be trashed. We walk into my room but everything that was important to me I took with me when I ran. I never had much to begin with so even my bedroom is pretty empty. I duck into the bathroom before moving on to the last room.

My father's bedroom.

I was never allowed inside it and I hesitate now before I slowly push the door open. His scent is stronger in here and I walk in, taking in the unmade bed and the piles of clothes on the floor. I don't want any of his clothes or furniture and I'm turning to leave when something catches my eyes. There's a book on his nightstand. It's old but I've never seen it before, which is weird because I read every book in this house at least a dozen times.

I walk closer and see that it's not a book at all but a diary. My father doesn't seem like the type to keep a diary or journal and my curiosity is piqued. I pick the book up, scanning the first couple of words and my breath catches in my throat.

"Salem? What is it?" Campbell asks as he makes his way towards me.

"It's a diary. My mother's diary." I say as I look up at him with wide eyes.

I flip through it and stop when I see one word. *Pregnancy*. She was writing this diary when she was pregnant with me. I lean against Campbell as I start to read.

January 16th

Dear Diary,

I'm officially in the third trimester! I'm so excited to have this baby and to be a mother. I can't wait to hold my little girl in my arms, to cuddle her and play with her. Vince feels the same. He is so sweet, always talking to my belly and rubbing it. Vince is even more protective now that I'm starting to show. You should see the way he runs around, making sure I have everything that I need. I know that he's going to be the best dad. Our little girl is going to be so lucky and she is already so loved. I can't wait for July to be here so that I can finally hold my little girl in my arms.

I don't realize I'm crying until Campbell is pulling me into his arms and wiping the tears from my face.

"What is it, princess?"

"That wasn't the father that I got." I sob into his chest.

I hand him the diary and he reads the passage I read while I curl into his side and cry. Campbell closes the diary when he's done and wraps both arms around me. He shushes me, rocking me back and forth as I cry for the family that I never got to have. For both of the parents that I lost the day that I was born.

CHAPTER TWELVE

Campbell

Salem has been quiet for the last couple of days and I don't know how to pull her out of it. I know grief after losing someone is normal but I still don't like seeing sad or upset. I've been letting her sleep in while I go out at dawn to work on the farm. We still haven't decided what to do with her father's house or land but I'm not in any rush. I don't want to push her before she's ready.

I finish up for the morning and head back to the house to eat lunch with Salem. We've been getting into a routine over the last couple of days and I'm amazed at how comfortably Salem fits into my life here. She's been settling in at the house and she started to move stuff around and decorate it the way that she likes.

I walk up to the house, expecting to find Salem curled up on the couch with her mother's diary. She's been reading it over and over again ever since she found it. I've read it too and the love that her mother and father obviously had for her is written on every page.

I had been thinking that Salem's grief was for the loss of her father but after talking with her about the diary I realize it's more than that. She's not just grieving her father's death but also the loss of what could have been. My parents have always been loving and supportive of me so it's hard for me to relate but I'm trying.

I walk into the house and look to the couch but find it empty. I make my way into the kitchen to find Salem at the stove. She's barefoot with her long hair braided and hanging over one shoulder. She's wearing one of her usual dresses that I love so much and as she turns to smile at me it flits around her thighs. She finally ordered some new clothes and they should be here any day now. I'm going to miss seeing her running around in her dresses but it will be nice to have her be able to come out to the barn with me. I've been dying to show her all of the land or to take her for a horseback ride.

I walk over to her, dropping a kiss on her lips as she smiles up at me. She wraps her arms around my neck and her fingers immediately find their way into my beard. It's gotten longer and I was wondering if I should trim it but she seems to like it and until she tells me otherwise, I'll just let it grow.

"You seem happy, princess." I comment as she leans up and kisses me.

I kiss her back and smile down at her. It's nice

to see her so happy again.

"Yeah, I think I finally got my head wrapped around everything."

"I'm happy to hear that Salem."

"Just... will you promise me something?"

"Anything, princess."

"If we have kids, and something happens to me, promise me that you'll never change and treat them the way that my father treated me."

"Of course, Salem. I'll love our kids, no matter what. I would never hurt them. I can promise that I will always protect them and treat them right."

She nods against me before wrapping her arms tighter around my waist. We hug for a minute before we break apart and she shows me what she made for lunch. She's been trying out more and more recipes and I can tell that she really likes to cook. She's been talking about these new copper pots and pans that she saw online and I ordered them to surprise her. They should be here today and I can't wait to see her face when she opens the box.

Today, she's made some kind of quiche with broccoli and ham and carrots. She made some kind of soup and a salad to go with it and it all smells delicious. I help her carry everything over to the table and she tells me about some new brownie recipe that she wants to try. She chatters on about some different recipes and asks if I've ever heard about this website called Pinterest. Apparently, it's an incredible place to find recipes. I smile at how sweet she is and add getting her a cell phone to my to-do list. Speaking of phones.

"My parents called. They're planning a trip up from Florida. They're pretty annoyed that they weren't here for the wedding. They're excited to finally meet you though."

Salem seems nervous and I lean over. "They're going to love you, princess. I promise."

She asks me questions about them while we eat and I tell her about how they already know all about her. I always told them that she was the girl that I was going to marry. She smiles at that and seems to be more relaxed about them coming.

We finish lunch and I help her with the dishes. We talk about our honeymoon again and finally narrow it down to two places. I'll leave that up her to decide; I don't care where we go as long as we're together.

"Have you decided what you want to do with the land? Or the house?" I ask carefully.

"Not yet. We need to tear the house down; it's not safe, but as for the rest... well, I'm still thinking about it."

I nod as she dries the last dish and I take it from her hands and put it away as she hangs up the dishtowel. I take her hand in mine and she follows me into the living room. I've been taking some time off in the afternoons so that we can spend more time together. Usually, we cuddle on the couch and watch tv or movies. Salem didn't get to do that when she was younger and I like watching her face while she watches classic Disney movies or old tv shows.

This time when I sit on the couch, Salem sits on my lap instead of the cushion next to mine. I'm a little surprised but totally welcome to this new sitting arrangement. We haven't had any other sexual adventures since her father died but it looks like with her grief passing, she's gotten her sex drive back.

She sits on my lap with her legs dangling over mine and her arms wrapped around my neck. She brings her face close to mine and I think that she's going to kiss me but she turns her face at the last minute and starts to kiss up and down my neck. I moan and my hands run up and down her legs, going higher each time, as her lips tease down my neck.

My fingers stroke high on her thighs, brushing under her dress and against her panties. She moans against my skin and before I can stop myself, I have her flat on her back on the couch under me. Her legs spread and wrap around my waist as I rock against her. My fingers work under her dress as hers go to my belt and she pulls it from the loops. Her little fingers attack my jeans and soon we're both desperately pulling at each other's clothes, our mouths pulling apart only long enough tug clothes over our heads.

As soon as we're both naked, Salem wraps her hand around my erection and steers it towards her wet sex. We both watch as I slowly sink inch after inch inside of her until I'm fully seated. We both groan as I start to move slowly but the feeling of having her wrapped around me again after so many days is too much and soon, I'm pounding into her, hard and fast, while her fingers dig into my shoulders and back.

I can feel her start to pulse around my length and I know that she's going to go off soon. *Thank god*, I think as I feel my own orgasm start to bear down on me. It only takes two more strokes and Salem starts to come, scratching her nails down my back while she screams my name. Seeing her pleasure pushes me higher and soon I'm following her over.

I pick her up and shift her in my lap as we both come down. She pants and leans against me, her eyes closed and her sooty lashes laying against her flushed cheeks. Her red lips are parted and I can feel her warm breath as it fans across my pecs. She sits up after a few minutes and smiles as she straddles my lap once again.

"Can we do that again?"

I smile as I pick her up and carry her to our bedroom.

CHAPTER THIRTEEN

Salem

Two Months Later...

    I finish throwing up my breakfast in the toilet, wiping my mouth off and standing back up to rinse out my mouth. I'm glad that Campbell is still outside. I wanted to surprise him with the news and my friend at the bakery said that it would take a couple of days to make the cake that I wanted. I'm a good cook but a terrible baker so I had to wait until she could finish it.

    I never would have been able to pull this off by myself. Luckily, Campbell has been taking me around town and introducing me to people. I've met a lot of nice folks in the last couple of weeks and everyone has been so welcoming to me.

I really like the owner of the bakery though. Karen is so nice and funny and we share recipes and talk on the phone and she brings me cookies and brownies every time I see her. She's the only person that I told about the pregnancy and she agreed to help me with my surprise.

Karen should be able to drop off the cake any minute now. I offered to go pick it up, Campbell got me a car and has been teaching me to drive and I just got my license last week. Karen said no though when she found out how bad my morning sickness has been. I had tried to argue with her but I'm grateful that she turned me down now.

I finish cleaning up and pull on a pair of jeans and a loose shirt. My new clothes finally came in and I want to laugh now as I think about how they won't fit in just a couple of months. I pad down to the kitchen to make myself some tea and the water is just starting to boil when there's a knock on the door. I squeal as I race to answer it and help Karen carry in the cake.

She did an amazing job and I gush about it to her. She refuses to let me pay, saying that friends do things for their friends. I smile and hug her tight before she slips out. She's been letting me come and work with her in the afternoon and I promise that I'll see her tomorrow for my shift. She hugs me one last time before she ducks out the door and drives off.

I set the cake on the counter before I pull out my cell phone sending a quick text to Campbell and asking him to come up to the house. He texts back after a minute saying he'll be right here and I smile as I wait for him to walk inside. I wonder if he's on the farm this morning or if he went over to my father's house to supervise the construction.

We finally decided what to do with my father's house and land and it's been under construction for the last month. The house was torn down and, in its place, we're building a library. There will be a big playground on the land next to the library and the rest of the land will be joined with Campbell's. The town will finally get a library and a bigger playground and the land will finally be used for something good. Plus, I'll get to work at the library and do what I love, read. I smile as I think about our kids playing on the playground there or curling up in the library with me and reading.

I hear the front door open and I step in front of the cake, hiding it as he walks into the kitchen.

"Hey, princess. What's going on?" He asks, confusion on his face.

"I have a surprise for you."

His eyes light up and I can see him looking me up and down. He's probably remembering the last surprise I had for him. I had gone shopping with Karen and we had stopped at this lingerie store. I came home and did a little fashion show for him. I made it through two outfits before he basically tackled me onto the bed.

"Not that kind of surprise!" I say as he steps closer.

"What is it then?" He asks with a slight pout.

"Close your eyes." I laugh.

He does as I ask and I step out of the way, walking over to his side.

"Ok, open them."

His eyes blink open and he takes in the sight before him. The cake is square and white with a pink and blue calendar on the top. There are little baby shoes on our due date, May 25th. Campbell gapes at the cake, his eyes as wide as saucers before he spins and swoops me up into his arms. He spins me around, whooping with excitement and as soon as he pulls back, I'm pushing away from him and rushing over to the trash can. I barely make it in time before I'm hurling once again.

"Oh, Salem! Shit, princess, I'm so sorry. I was just excited." He says as he holds my hair back.

I finish being sick and stand back up. "It's ok. I'm glad you were excited." I laugh.

He kisses my forehead before getting me a glass of water and carrying me over to the table. My stomach is already settling and I take a couple of sips of the water. Campbell rubs my back until he's sure I'm ok.

"So, we're pregnant!" I say when I'm finally composed.

Campbell laughs.

"Are you happy?" I ask when he just smiles at me.

"I'm over the moon, princess." He says as he

pulls me into his lap.

"I love you so much, princess."

"I love you, too."

He kisses me but pulls back before things can get too heated, probably still worried about me getting sick. Campbell starts laughing and I look at him, confused.

"Maybe we should build another house on your father's land." I cock my head at him, wondering why he would want that.

"My parents are going to be so happy. They're going to end up moving back here."

I laugh as I realize he's right. I met Campbell's mom and dad last month when they came up to visit and I loved them instantly. They're so warm and loving, nothing like my father. They were already asking about grandbabies when they were here last month and I know they'll be thrilled when we tell them the news. We both laugh as we picture telling them the news. When we calm down, I stroke my hand down Campbell's beard, staring into his eyes.

"We're going to be parents, Campbell."

"I know, princess. You're going to be a great mom."

I smile as Campbell tells me exactly what I needed to hear. I already know that he'll be the best dad and I can't wait to start our family together.

CHAPTER FOURTEEN

Campbell

Ten Years Later...

I watch as Salem and our kids curl up in the reading nook. She's reading to them from some book series that they all got hooked on and the kids are all hanging on her every word. I hate to interrupt but if I don't stop them, then they will read all day. They all can get lost in a book and let the day pass them by. Salem definitely passed her love for books down to our children.

We had three kids, all within five years. Two boys, Sam and Caleb, and then our little girl, Ariel. We decided that three was enough for us and, although my parents would have liked more grandkids, it was perfect for us. My parents ended up moving back up, just like I knew they would. We built them a little house on our land and they help Salem out with the library and both of us with the kids.

The library and playground were finished right after Salem gave birth to Sam and we opened it a month after that. Salem loves being a librarian and helping others find a perfect book to get lost in and I love that she's happy. I also love that she's so close by. I can pop over whenever I want and steal a few minutes with my wife.

I'm still working the farm and I'm happy to see that my kids have taken an interest in it too. Right now, they mostly just like the animals. You can't drag Ariel away from the horses and I swear she would be riding them all day if you let her. Sam and Caleb both like the animals but their newfound interest is riding around on the tractors and other equipment. We spend most Sunday's all out in the barn together and they're my favorite days. Watching my girls with the horses and teaching my boys about how the farm works makes me happier than anything. I'm looking forward to passing the farm on to them when they're older just like my parents did for me.

Tonight though, I'm just looking forward to taking my wife out on a date. It's our anniversary and I arranged for my parents to watch the kids for the night. Salem and I are going to a fancy dinner in the city and then are spending a night at a hotel. Karen and her husband have been raving about some new restaurant that just opened and they tried last month and I know that Salem has been dying to try it too so I made us reservations. If we don't leave soon though, we will miss that reservation.

"Alright, guys." I say as I walk up to them. "It's time to head to Grandma and Grandpa's."

The kids all smile and hop up. They love staying with their grandparents, probably because they spoil them rotten. I know my mother has been baking sweets up all day, anticipating their arrival tonight. I smile as they hug each of us and tell us to have fun before they run out past us. I pull Salem up and help her finish putting the loose books away before we head to the door, waving goodbye to the evening librarian.

We walk hand in hand back home and she tries to get what we're doing out of me the whole way. I just smile and pull her along faster. She laughs as we practically run the last few yards and we stumble up the stairs. I catch her and lead her into the house. She tells me she'll be ready in half an hour and I take a seat on the couch as I hear the shower start.

True to her word, she's dressed and ready half an hour later. I hear her heels clicking as she makes her way down the hallway and I stand as they get closer. Then I almost fall back onto the sofa when she comes into view.

Even after all these years, she is still the most beautiful woman that I have ever seen. She's wearing a tight hot pink dress that molds to all of her curves. Her hair is pulled back on wide side and held in place with some kind of clip and strappy black heels complete the look. She is perfection.

"You're gorgeous, princess." I say as she walks over to me.

"Thanks, Campbell." She says as I take her hand and help her into the truck.

We make the drive to the city in under an hour, beating all of the rush hour traffic. Salem tells me about her day and asks me what I did as we drive and finally, we pull up outside the restaurant. We park and walk the half block to the doors and when she sees where we're going, she squeals and pulls on my arm, urging me to move faster. I laugh but oblige and soon we're inside and being seated.

Salem spends the meal talking about how nice the restaurant is, all of the décor, and moaning over the food. I'll admit, the food is good but I would still take a home-cooked meal from Salem any day. We finish up at the restaurant and I pay the bill before taking her hand in mine and leading her back to the truck.

"Thanks, Campbell. That was a great anniversary." She says, kissing my cheek.

"It's not over yet, princess." I say as I steer back into traffic and head for our hotel.

We pull up outside a couple of minutes later and I grab the small overnight bag I hid in the backseat. I take her hand and she smiles at me as we walk inside and check-in. She wraps her arms around my waist as we ride the elevator up to our floor. I find our room and slide the keycard, opening the door and letting Salem walk in first.

She walks in and looks around, poking her head into the bathroom as she goes. The room is large and decorated in creams and golds. It's nice looking and relaxing and I hope that Salem likes it. She spins around and smiles at me.

"Mr. McConnely! You really went all out this year." She says as she makes her way across the floor towards me.

My eyes are transfixed by the subtle sway of her hips and before I know it, she's in front of me. Her hands wrap around my waist and she leans up on her toes to kiss me. As soon as her lips meet mine, her fingers are in my beard. Even after all these years she still can't seem to get enough of it.

Our tongues tangle and I walk her back towards the

bed as she starts to pull at my clothes. Having three small kids means that we've gotten really good at the quickie sex. I have to force myself to slow my hands and when Salem's fingers still frantically pull at my clothes, I pull away.

"We don't have to rush, princess. We have all night remember? We can take our time."

"It's been too long. I need you now, Campbell. Right now, I just want it hard and fast. I want to scream your name and not have to hold back or worry about one of the kids hearing us. We have all night so you can fuck me slow next time."

She blinks her blue eyes clouded with lust up at me and just like when we met, I am powerless to deny her anything. We pull our clothes off quickly and she pushes me down onto the bed before coming down after me. I take her fast and hard the first time and then the fourth and fifth time and eventually, Salem passes out on top of me with a happy smile on her face.

I kiss her forehead and think about how lucky I am that I went walking in the woods all of those years ago. I found my princess, my best friend, my wife, and partner. I don't know what I would do or where I would be without her but luckily, I don't need to find out.

THE END.

ALSO BY SHAW HART

CONNECT WITH ME!

If you enjoyed this story, please consider leaving a review on Amazon or any other reader sire of blog that you like. Don't forget to recommend it to your other reader friends. If you want to chat with me, please consider joining my VIP list or connecting with me on one of my Social Media platforms. I love talking with each of my readers. Links below!

● Follow me on Facebook

● Follow Shaw Hart on Bookbub

● Join my private reader group, Shaw Hart Bookies

● Join my VIP list

● Follow me on Instagram

Printed in Great Britain
by Amazon